Wendy's Weather Warriors

Tornado Trouble

by Kathryn Lay   illustrated by Jason Wolff

magic Wagon

visit us at www.abdopublishing.com

To Richard, my own Weather Warrior. You are my encouragement, my joy, builder of my hope— you are my husband, my love and my best friend— KL

Printed in the United States of America, Melrose Park, Illinois.
022010
092010

 This book contains at least 10% recycled materials.

Text by Kathryn Lay
Illustrations by Jason Wolff
Edited by Stephanie Hedlund and Rochelle Baltzer
Cover and interior design by Abbey Fitzgerald

Library of Congress Cataloging-in-Publication Data

Lay, Kathryn.
   Tornado trouble / by Kathryn Lay ; illustrated by Jason Wolff.
      p. cm.
   Includes bibliographical references and index.
   ISBN 978-1-60270-754-2 (alk. paper)
   1. Tornadoes--Juvenile literature. I. Wolff, Jason, ill. II. Title.
   QC955.2.L39 2010
      551.55'3--dc22   2009048843

CONTENTS

CHAPTER 1

Wild About Weather

Wendy Peters stepped through the doors of Circleville Elementary. It was her first day in a new school in this new town. It was a little scary. But when she walked into Mr. Andrews's classroom, she knew it was going to be a fun year.

There were stations all around the room for social studies, reading, math, and science. She clapped her hands when she saw the weather poster in the science station. She bet no one in her class knew as much about weather as she did.

"Welcome!" Mr. Andrews said when everyone was seated. He was tall with blond hair pulled back in a ponytail. He smiled at the class. A golden hamster sat in his hand, its nose twitching.

The girl sitting next to Wendy leaned toward her. "We're lucky," she said. "They say Mr. Andrews is the coolest teacher in fifth grade. Maybe even the coolest in the whole school!"

Wendy grinned. "I can tell. I'm Wendy Peters. I just moved here. I used to live in the Texas Hill Country. Now my dad says we live in the panhandle of Texas."

"I'm Jessica Roberts," the girl said. She tossed her long, dark hair over her shoulders and blew at the bangs falling over her eyes. "I've lived here my whole life. I can't wait until we get to the science station."

She quickly drew on her notebook and held it up to show Wendy. Wendy squinted through her glasses. It was a picture of a cloud with raindrops falling.

Wendy smiled. Maybe she wasn't the only one in Mr. Andrews's class who liked weather.

That morning, Mr. Andrews led them to the different learning stations. In social studies, they learned about map skills. At the reading station, Mr. Andrews drew names and a boy named Dennis Galloway got to pick the first book to read. Wendy clapped when he chose a book about a weather station in Alaska.

It wasn't until after lunch that Mr. Andrews said, "Time to move to the science station."

Wendy sat beside Jessica on the floor.

There were posters of animal skeletons and plants. A bottle of seeds sat next to a stack of small plastic pots for planting. One shelf was lined with cages and aquariums.

Mr. Andrews also sat on the floor. "What part of science will we start with this year?"

Wendy's hand shot into the air. A girl wearing overalls shouted, "The ocean!"

"Rocks," someone else said.

Wendy called out, "Weather!"

A boy with in a striped shirt groaned. He shoved Dennis and said, "Oh no, not another one."

Wendy wondered what he meant. Then Jessica raised her hand. "I vote for weather, too."

Dennis pulled a notebook from his back pocket. "I have experiments for any type of weather. We could make a tornado and a rain gauge and create lightning and make snow and . . ."

Mr. Andrews nodded. "Very exciting, Dennis." He pointed to the poster on the wall. Inside big circles on the poster were pictures of lightning, tornadoes, hail, and more. "I had planned a weather unit for next month, but maybe we could do it early. What should we start with?"

Wendy raised her hand again. "My dad is a storm spotter."

A boy by Dennis laughed. "He paints spots on storms?"

Dennis folded his arms. "No, Austin. That means he goes out in storms and looks for tornadoes and stuff and tells the weather service so they can warn people."

"That sounds scary," a girl said.

Mr. Andrews wiggled his eyebrows. "Yes, it is a little scary, Tanya. But it's very important and helps a lot of people get information so they can stay safe."

Wendy stared at her classmates. Couldn't they see how exciting weather could be? "I've been studying the weather service's predictions for our area this year," she shared. "They're expecting us to have a late severe storm season. Maybe even tornadoes!"

Mr. Andrews agreed they would talk about tornadoes during science station time that first week.

"For homework, I want everyone to bring a word used with tornadoes to class tomorrow," Mr. Andrews announced. "Tell us the word and what it means."

Wendy could think of a long list of words. Which one should she pick? She could tell she was going to love Mr. Andrews's class.

After school, Wendy walked beside Jessica as they followed their teacher outside to wait for the buses.

"Do you want to come to my house?" Wendy asked. "We could talk about our homework. And, I have a surprise at my house. Especially if you like weather."

Jessica rubbed at the freckles on her nose. "That would be great!"

Dennis stood in line behind them.

"Hey, I'm a weather nut, too," he said. "Can I come?"

Wendy thought a minute. "Sure! I didn't have any friends at my last school who loved weather stuff like me."

Dennis nodded. "Yeah, no one in my class last year liked it. They used to call me *Mr. Weather Kid.*" He crossed his eyes and Wendy laughed.

Jessica and Dennis agreed to ask their parents if they could come over after dinner.

Wendy couldn't wait to show them her weather station in her backyard. She bet no one else in school had their own weather station. Maybe Jessica and Dennis could come over every day and talk about weather.

She snapped her fingers. She had an idea. A great idea.

CHAPTER 2

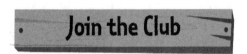

Join the Club

"**W**ould you please stop bouncing around?" Wendy's mother said.

Wendy skipped around the living room with Cumulus barking and dancing around her. Wendy laughed when the black-and-white Schnoodle hopped on his hind legs as if trying to copy her.

"I can't help it, I'm excited!" Wendy shouted.

Her mother sighed, then laughed and did a little skip toward the front door when the doorbell rang.

Wendy ran past her mother. "I got it!"

"Hi, Dennis," she said when she opened the door.

Dennis stepped inside with a backpack slung over his shoulder. There were glow-in-the-dark stickers of clouds all over it. A tornado and raindrops had been drawn with black marker.

By the time his parents had introduced themselves to Wendy's parents and left, the doorbell rang again.

"Jessica!" Wendy yelled, pulling her new friend into the house. Jessica's father was a newspaper reporter, and he told Wendy's father he wanted to interview him about being a storm spotter.

"Let's go out to the backyard to my weather station," Wendy said.

Jessica adjusted her backpack. "You have a weather station in your backyard?"

Wendy laughed. "Well, it's really someone's old clubhouse, but I call it Wendy's House of Weather. My dad and I fixed it up when we moved in this summer."

On the way through the kitchen, Wendy grabbed three juice boxes from the refrigerator. Then, she led her new friends out the back door.

"Wow," Dennis said. "That is monstrous cool!"

Wendy grinned. "Thanks." She let Dennis and Jessica explore the outside of the remodeled clubhouse. They tapped the thermometer and peered into the rain gauge.

Wendy walked inside and said, "Welcome to Wendy's House of Weather."

Just as Dennis and Jessica stepped inside, Cumulus burst out the back door.

"Cumulus is going to go nuts if you don't let him come," Wendy's mother said.

"Cumulus loves attention," Wendy said. While Cumulus bounced around their feet, Wendy showed her new friends around.

Wendy pointed to a box sitting on an old wooden desk. "This was my dad's old ham radio. He got a new one last Christmas, so I get to use this one," Wendy explained.

"Wow, you know how to use it?" Dennis asked. He sat down at the desk and picked up the microphone.

Wendy nodded. "Yeah, I talk with my dad when he's out checking the weather. Sometimes I talk to his storm chasing friends, too. It can either be really boring out there or really exciting."

Wendy walked to the other side of the room. "Here's the barometer I got for my birthday."

Dennis tapped the barometer. "I used to have one of these, but my cousin dropped it. Right before a storm hit, I would watch the air pressure drop. Boing!"

Dennis grinned. He picked up a small

radio. "That's a nice weather radio. I've got one, too."

Jessica nodded. "Me too."

"Wow," Dennis said. He pointed at the poster on the wall. In big letters at the top of the poster were the words *Enhanced Fujita Tornado Scale*.

"I bought this when my dad took me to the weather station in Oklahoma. See, it shows the different levels of tornadoes from F0 through F5."

Jessica pulled out a small digital camera and started snapping pictures. "Someday I'm going to be a famous storm photographer," she said.

Dennis jumped up. "I have an anemometer at home."

Jessica scrunched her nose. "That sounds made up. I've never heard of it."

Wendy's jaw dropped. "You call yourself a weather nut and you don't know what an anemometer is? It measures wind speed."

Dennis spun around the room, making whooshing sounds.

Jessica shrugged. "Well, I don't know everything about weather. I just think it's cool and I love to take pictures of clouds and lightning and stuff."

She snapped a picture of Wendy and the barometer.

Wendy showed them the rest the weather house. She pointed out her bookshelf full of weather books, the calendar with pictures of tornadoes and lightning storms, and the award she got at her last school for her cloud report.

"That's when we got Cumulus," she said, giving the dog a hug.

Wendy watched Jessica and Dennis as they studied her weather house. It was time to tell them her great idea.

"Let's start a club," she announced.

Dennis's eyes widened. "A club?"

"Yeah," Wendy said. "A weather club. We can meet here after school and on weekends. And we can help Mr. Andrews tell everyone about weather and . . . well, we could do lots of stuff."

Jessica was trying to pose Cumulus for a picture. She whirled around. "Wow, I'm in. I'll be the official club photographer."

Dennis said, "Count me in, too. I'll be the weather scientist. I have a book full of cool weather experiments."

Wendy held out her hands, palms up. When Jessica and Dennis gave her a high five, she said, "Great. Our first order of business is to decide which tornado terms we'll take to school tomorrow."

CHAPTER 3

Danger

Something wet tickled Wendy's nose. She'd been dreaming that everyone in school wanted to join her weather club. She opened her eyes to see Cumulus on her pillow.

Wendy jumped out of bed and hugged Cumulus.

"It's time for school!" she shouted as she grabbed her glasses off the table beside her bed. Cumulus barked and chased his tail.

"I wish you could come. Mr. Andrews is great. And I can't wait for science today." She had her word to share. Well, it was actually two words—wall cloud.

And even more exciting, she and Dennis and Jessica worked on a notebook all about tornadoes and tornado safety. She hoped there would be time to read it in class.

"Please move to the science station," Mr. Andrews said after lunch. Sneakers the Hamster was sitting on Mr. Andrews's shoulder, sniffing at the teacher's ear.

When everyone was sitting at the science station, Mr. Andrews said, "Who'd like to share their tornado word?"

Austin jumped up and shouted, "Hail!"

Someone gasped. "Ooh, Mr. Andrews, he said a bad word in class!"

Wendy folded her arms. "No, he didn't. He means the balls of ice that can come at the end of a bad thunderstorm . . . sometimes before a tornado hits!"

Austin's mouth dropped open. "Yeah, that's what I meant." He gave Wendy a surprised smile.

Mr. Andrews nodded. "Good. What else?"

Everyone began shouting words until Mr. Andrews asked them to raise their hands first. By the time they were done, they had funnel, rotation, twister, rope, wedge, debris, and green.

"Green?" Austin asked.

"Clouds can look green when a storm might have tornadoes in it," Dennis explained.

Mr. Andrews smiled. "Everyone did a good job."

Wendy cleared her throat. "We . . . I mean Jessica, Dennis, and I . . . we made a booklet all about tornado safety and stuff. Can I read it?"

She held out the thick notebook.

"Well, it's a little long for class today. But maybe you could type it out and make copies for everyone."

Wendy looked at Jessica and Dennis. "Sure, we'll do it," she said when they nodded.

After school, Wendy asked her mom if they could walk through the school before they went home.

"Sure, but why?" her mom asked.

"You'll see," Wendy replied.

Up and down the halls they walked. Wendy peeked into rooms and bathrooms. There were a lot of glass windows. The cafeteria was all glass on one side. It was also used for an auditorium. It was the only room big enough for everyone at the same time.

"Most of the classrooms are against outside walls," she told her mom.

"You're right. I think I see what you're doing," her mother said.

Wendy snapped her fingers. She pulled out a notebook and began to make notes for their club meeting that afternoon.

Then, Wendy marched into the office and straight to the school secretary. "I'd like to see the school's severe weather plan please," she said politely.

The secretary stopped stapling papers and peered over her glasses at Wendy. "I don't believe we have one, young lady," she said.

Wendy's mouth dropped open. "Doesn't the principal realize that everyone in the school is in danger?"

She turned and stormed out of the office. It was up to the weather club to warn Principal Stuard.

CHAPTER 4

Stormy Ideas

Wendy's mom peeked inside the weather club. "Here are a few snacks for your friends." She held out a tray with three cups of hot chocolate mix, a kettle of hot water, a bag of mini-marshmallows, and some graham crackers.

Wendy started to tell her that it was 68 degrees outside and a little warm for hot chocolate. But, she didn't want to hurt her mother's feelings.

"Thanks," she said instead.

Her mother smiled. Then, she set the tray on a card table in the middle of the room and left.

As soon as Jessica and Dennis showed up Wendy said, "We have to warn everyone at school."

Dennis stuffed a handful of marshmallows into his mouth and mumbled, "Warn them? About what? About the fact that there's hardly any meat in the meat loaf?"

Wendy shook her head. "About the fact that the school has no plan for what to do if a tornado struck."

"Knock, knock, anyone home?" a voice called. "Just wanted to say hello to your new friends."

"Dad, this is Dennis. He's really into weather experiments and stuff. And Jessica wants to be a photographer," Wendy said.

"Weather photographer," Jessica added.

Her father stooped and bent his tall legs as he walked through the door. "It's great to meet you both. Glad Wendy found some more weather weirdos like us." He grinned at them.

"We need your help, Dad," Wendy said. Her father squatted down beside them and listened as Wendy told them about what she had discovered in the school.

"In our old school, there was a plan posted in every room," she said. "And in the halls and cafeteria and . . ."

Dennis pulled out his notebook of experiments. "I could make a fake tornado and scare everybody and then they would see that there needs to be a plan."

Wendy's father whistled. "That would have to be some amazing fake tornado. If you educate the leaders first, they'll pass the information to everyone."

Jessica snapped a picture of Wendy's father. "You mean like the principal?"

"Yes," he said. "And then the teachers. They can each tell their students what the safety plan would be. Safety in severe weather is important, and that's why storm spotters do what we do."

Wendy hugged her dad. "Great idea!"

Her father ducked back out the door as Wendy, Dennis, and Jessica worked on a plan. They studied photographs that Jessica took of the school. They drew a map of the school, circled the dangerous spots, and put big red X's in the safe places.

"X marks the spots!" Dennis said.

The next day at school, they told Mr. Andrews their ideas for making sure the students would be safe. The teacher walked over to the aquarium where Bob the Boa lived and took out the snake while the kids in charge of cleaning the aquarium worked.

"It's true, I don't think we've ever discussed a severe weather plan at school," he said. "The four of us will talk with Mrs. Stuard about it."

"I know all about tornado safety," Wendy explained. "And I know where we can be safe at Circleville."

"And I can look up photographs of tornado damage on the school computer and print them out," Jessica said.

"Those are helpful ideas," Mr. Andrews told them. Bob's tongue slithered in and out. "I'll give you until tomorrow to figure out what each of you will say."

Wendy put on her most serious expression. But her stomach was doing jumping jacks. Would the principal listen to three kids?

During science, Mr. Andrews talked about severe storms and what makes for perfect tornado weather.

"What helps create a tornado?" he asked.

Wendy's hand shot into the air. "Wind shears."

Austin said, "My mom uses shears to cut things." He used two fingers to make a cutting motion.

"Not scissors, goofy," Dennis said. "It's sort of like a hose in your garden."

"Huh?" Austin asked. "Do I use the scissors to cut the hose?"

Dennis shook his head. "No, a wind shear happens when the wind moves from different directions and different parts of the atmosphere."

Wendy was amazed at Dennis. He reminded her of this science guy on television who could talk about anything.

"The air rolls up like the shape of a coiled water hose," Dennis explained. "So when a storm comes and has a big updraft of wind, it picks up the rolling air and twists it down and . . . ta-da! A tornado."

Mr. Andrews nodded. "Good explanation of a wind shear, Dennis. Now, I'd like to—"

Dennis raised his hand. "And talking about wind, if we had a paper plate and paper cups and some colored tape and a thumbtack and a pencil and some double-sided tape and a stopwatch, I could show you how to measure wind speed." He let out his breath.

Wendy let hers out, too. She didn't know anyone could say that much in one breath.

Mr. Andrews patted Dennis on the back. "Sounds like fun. Make me a list of what we need."

Wendy glanced out the classroom windows. It was muggy and sticky for mid-September and the sky seemed to have more clouds building up. In the west, she could see outlines of clouds that looked like heavy smoke piled up high.

Wendy couldn't wait to get home and check the weather forecasts for the next few days. She didn't like how still everything seemed, like the calm before a storm.

"We've got the Welcome Back to School program in two days. Maybe Mrs. Stuard will let us meet with the teachers and have a drill next week," Mr. Andrews said.

Wendy glanced out the window again, then at Dennis and Jessica.

"Sooner might be better," she said. "Much sooner."

CHAPTER 5

A Warning

Wendy sat in the clubhouse and waited for Jessica and Dennis. She had called an emergency meeting as soon as she looked at the weather maps on her dad's computer.

Cumulus crawled into her lap and whimpered.

"It's okay, boy," she said, rubbing his curly head. A day or two before a big storm, Cumulus never left her side. He paced in circles and sniffed the air.

Would Mrs. Stuard agree to have a planning meeting with the teachers right away? Wendy was afraid the principal would want to wait until after the first school assembly.

"We can't wait," Wendy told Cumulus. "We have to convince the principal to do it tomorrow."

Something flashed in her eyes.

"Great shot," Jessica said. "You looked like you were thinking something important."

Wendy blinked until the spots went away. "I was thinking."

"Now you're blinking," Dennis said. He set his backpack carefully on the card table in the middle of the room, then held out a dog treat. Cumulus gave his hand a quick lick and grabbed the treat.

"What's in the bag?" Wendy asked.

Dennis opened his backpack. "Stuff to show Mr. Andrews. All kinds of great experiments and projects we can do in class. A tornado in a bottle, a homemade anemometer to measure wind speed, and—"

"That's great Dennis, but before we have some weather fun, we've got to get the school ready for trouble," Wendy cut in.

"Trouble?" Jessica asked.

"Tornado trouble," Wendy said. "I can't be sure, of course, but everything I've been hearing on the news and showing on my weather instruments looks kind of scary."

"This is KCWS93W calling for StormGirl. Are you there?" a ghostly voice said.

Jessica jumped. Wendy laughed. "It's the ham radio. One of my storm friends is calling."

Wendy ran to the radio and picked up the microphone. "This is KWP9S. I'm here. Is that you, Weathermouth?" She turned to Dennis and Jessica. "He's a meteorologist at a small radio station."

"That's me. Listen, just wanted to make sure you were keeping watch on your weather over there. There could be some big storms heading your way in the next twenty-four to forty-eight hours."

Wendy held down the button on her microphone. "Yeah, I've been watching that. We're talking to our principal

tomorrow about a weather safety plan at school. They don't have one yet."

The radio speaker filled with static for a moment. "Sorry about that, a bit of lightning. Listen, get your school ready. I don't like the look of what's coming. Tell your dad to come see me sometime."

"Thanks for the warning," Wendy gasped. "I'll tell him."

She shook the microphone at her friends. "I told you we might be heading for trouble."

Cumulus put his nose in the air and let out a howl.

CHAPTER 6

Tornado Drill

Mr. Andrews told teacher jokes to the school secretary while they waited to see the principal the next morning.

"One day this kid says to his teacher, 'I don't think I deserved a zero on my homework.' The teacher says, 'I agree, but that's the lowest grade I could give you.'"

Wendy looked at Jessica and rolled her eyes toward the ceiling while Dennis laughed out loud.

"Good one, Mr. Andrews," Dennis said.

The school secretary smiled. Everyone loved to joke with Mr. Andrews. Wendy was glad she was in his class. Another teacher might not be so ready to believe them about rushing the principal to get the school storm safety plan ready. Another teacher might not make class so fun for weather nuts like her and Dennis and Jessica.

The secretary's phone rang. She picked it up and listened a moment, then smiled at Wendy. "You can all go into Mrs. Stuard's office now."

Wendy took a deep breath. "Let's go," she said.

Dennis pulled out his notebook. "Maybe we could start with a little weather experiment to get her in the mood?" he suggested.

Mr. Andrews led the way to the back of the offices. Wendy had never been into the principal's office here before. She'd been lots at her old school. Not because she was in trouble, but because her old principal and her dad had been storm spotting buddies.

"Come in and sit down," Mrs. Stuard said when they stood at her office door.

Wendy and her friends squeezed into a large, cushioned chair.

"I've been reading over your plan, Wendy. The last two years I meant to put together a storm safety plan, but, well, sometimes you put things off. Even adults."

Wendy nodded. "My mom says my dad puts off washing his favorite shirt as long as he can."

Jessica giggled.

Mrs. Stuard said, "I've given copies of your suggestions to each of the teachers. Next week we'll have a drill like we do fire drills."

Wendy leaned forward. "But Mrs. Stuard, next week might be too late."

"Too late?" Mrs. Stuard asked.

Dennis stood up and unzipped his backpack. "Weathermouth says there's bad weather coming. I could show you three or four weather experiments about tornadoes and big storms." He started piling empty soda bottles, tubes, and bottles of sand on her desk.

Mrs. Stuard's eyes widened. "Uh, well, Dennis, I'd be happy to look at them some other time, but I'm very busy right now with the assembly tomorrow. There's my speech to prepare, the play rehearsal to look over, the choir to listen to once more . . ."

Wendy jumped up, nearly knocking Mr. Andrews over. "Please, Mrs. Stuard. Couldn't we have a quick drill today? Or have the teachers take a few minutes to tell everyone in their classes what to do in a weather emergency?"

Mrs. Stuard opened her mouth as if to protest, but then she met Wendy's eyes.

She looked at Dennis, who held out his backpack of gadgets, and at Jessica, who waved tornado pictures at the principal.

Mr. Andrews cleared his throat. "Selena, I don't think it'll take much time to do a quick drill. I've heard reports that we could be in for some severe weather over the next day or so."

Mrs. Stuard nodded. "Alright, I'll make an announcement and we'll do it after lunch."

Dennis promised Mrs. Stuard he'd bring his weather radio to school the next day.

By the time lunch was over, Wendy, Jessica, and Dennis had passed the word around the cafeteria about the drill that afternoon. Everyone was more excited about the chance to miss part of class.

Wendy watched the clock while Mr. Andrews talked about reading bar graphs in math. Just as the clock struck one o'clock, the speaker crackled.

"In a moment," Mrs. Stuard said, "there will be a long bell that will signal us as if there was an approaching severe storm. You will move into the hall and follow the duck and cover procedure your teacher has explained. Please exit your room in an orderly way."

Everyone in Mr. Andrews's class began talking at once.

The teacher tapped his ruler on his head as a signal for everyone to be quiet. "When the bell rings, I want today's class monitor to open the door. Starting with the row closest to the door, line up and walk outside the room. Line up against the hall walls to your right and squat on the floor. Put your heads down and cover them with your arms."

"What if the hall blows away?" Austin asked. "What if we blow away?"

"Should we all hold hands in case we do?" Lisa asked, smiling at Austin.

"Yuck," Austin said. "I'm going to hide under my desk."

Dennis snorted. "You'll get sucked out the window."

Wendy raised her hand. "I . . . we've studied the school and the hall is the safest place to go. We're not against an outside wall or near any windows. Look at all the stuff in here that could hit us if it gets blown around."

Mr. Andrews nodded. "Wendy's right. Now—"

At that moment, the bell rang. It was a long ring that seemed to go on and on.

"It's a tornado!" Austin screamed.

"It's a drill," Jessica said.

Mr. Andrews waited next to the door as everyone in class formed a line and walked out the door. Wendy sat in the hall between Jessica and Lisa.

The other classes sat against the walls, too. The teachers reminded everyone to duck their heads and cover them with their arms.

Wendy smiled to herself under her arms. Now the school was safe. They were ready for the bad weather that she knew was heading their way.

In the clubhouse that night, Dennis played tug-of-war with Cumulus. The dog growled and pulled at the Frisbee in his mouth. Dennis growled back.

"That was a good weather drill," Jessica said as she snapped a picture of the tug-of-war game.

Wendy nodded. "Yep. But it was only our first one. I just hope everyone remembers what to do in case these storms coming in tomorrow turn really bad."

She pointed to the small television screen next to the ham radio. Dennis had brought it from his room so they could make notes of what the meteorologist had to say.

" . . . thunderstorms likely with strong winds, possible hail, and potential for tornadoes . . ."

Wendy stepped outside the clubhouse. Dennis dragged Cumulus outside with him.

"Wow, look at the anemometer go!" he said.

The metal discs spun faster with the wind.

Wendy looked up. The sky was clear, but in the distance she could see clouds building. They weren't that far away.

Cumulus put his nose in the air and sniffed. He rubbed his head against Wendy's leg and whimpered.

CHAPTER 7

Stormy Weather

Mr. Andrews put the Sneakers the hamster, back into his cage and clapped his hands.

"Quiet, everyone. We'll be heading to the cafetorium for the assembly in a few minutes. Remember, be polite to the speakers. Applaud the choir and all the performers. They have worked hard to put on this year's first assembly."

Austin jumped up and made growling noises. "I could've been a great lion in the assembly if they'd asked me."

Dennis laughed. That made Austin roar even louder.

Mr. Andrews smiled. "If they need lions, I'm sure they'll ask you next time."

Wendy squirmed in her seat. She couldn't decide if she was more excited about the assembly or afraid about the weather.

"I'm going to try out for the choir next week," she whispered to Jessica. "I love to sing. My old school didn't have a choir that got to sing in assemblies."

Thunder exploded and someone screamed. Then, a bunch of kids screamed for the fun of it.

Wendy looked out the windows. Dark clouds moved closer to the school. A streak of lightning danced through the clouds.

"Mr. Andrews, I think we should turn on Dennis's weather radio," Wendy said.

Dennis jumped out of his chair and pulled the small, black radio from his backpack. With a nod from Mr. Andrews, Dennis turned it on.

An electronic voice said, "You are listening to NOAA all hazards weather radio. A severe thunderstorm warning and tornado watch has been issued for the counties of Bollin, Tarrant, Dyson, and Clairmont . . ."

"Hey, Dyson County. That's us!" Austin shouted.

Wendy wished she had her barometer with her. Was it dropping? What did it feel like outside? Was it going suddenly still? Did the birds stop singing? Would she be able to see a wall cloud forming from the cafetorium window?

Mr. Andrews looked at his watch. "It's time to line up for the assembly. Mrs. Stuard is aware of the weather."

Wendy raised her hand. "I think we should take Dennis's weather radio with us to the assembly."

Dennis waved the radio in the air. "I can fix it so it will only go off when there's a warning."

"That's a good idea, but let me take charge of it," Mr. Andrews said. "I want the volume turned low."

They filed down the hall to the cafetorium. Most of the kids from the other classes were already seated. Wendy watched the rain pelting on the glass windows.

"Tornadoes come from the west," Wendy said.

Austin turned in his seat and wrinkled his nose at her. "Big deal, I moved here from South Dakota."

Wendy sighed. "You're weird," she told him.

Just as the choir walked onstage, small pieces of hail beat against the windows.

CHAPTER 8

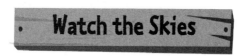
Watch the Skies

"**C**ircleville Elementary, we love you,

Circleville Elementary, we will be true,

A place to learn, a place to grow Circleville is the school to go!"

Wendy looked up at the front of the cafetorium where the choir stood in rows on the stage. She leaned forward and imagined herself standing in the front row, singing a solo.

Just as the choir sang the last note of their welcome back to school song (written and composed by Mrs. Fenner, the music teacher, they announced), a crack of thunder exploded.

Wendy jumped as several kids around her screamed. The lights flickered. There were more screams until Mrs. Stuard shushed everyone. Wendy could see that she was holding a weather radio.

The choir went back to singing, but Wendy had trouble watching them. Her eyes kept straying to the rain pouring outside the windows and the dark clouds that were turning green.

She nudged Dennis. "Look, green clouds. And look at that wind!"

He leaned across her to look out the windows. "Hope we don't see any cows flying by."

Jessica giggled. "I'd like to get a picture of that."

Austin leaned across Dennis and said, "Cows? How about an elephant? I'd sure like to see an elephant fly."

Mr. Andrews put his fingers to his lips and pointed to the stage. The choir walked back to their seats. Mrs. Stuard led everyone in applauding them as she moved to the microphone.

"Welcome, everyone, to a new year at Circleville Elementary. We have an exciting year planned and lots of new faces. Our new librarian, Mr. Cobbey, will be speaking in a moment about some of the programs he has planned for the next month."

Wendy wondered if Mr. Cobbey had any new books on weather. She glanced out the windows and gasped. Sunlight streamed inside the windows.

"Yay!" Tanya Ford shouted. "The rain stopped."

The sky looked almost yellow in the strange light. The trees outside the school had been almost bent over in the wind. Now they were still, not a leaf moving.

"This isn't good," Wendy whispered.

Austin snorted. "You're nuts. There's not even any wind anymore."

"Exactly," Dennis muttered.

Just as Wendy reached over and tapped Mr. Andrews's shoulder, a loud siren blared from somewhere outside.

At the same time, both Mr. Andrews's and Mrs. Stuard's weather radios beeped.

Wendy stared out the glass windows.

"Look!" someone shouted.

Wendy had already seen the dark funnel that had dipped from the clouds. It was thin and seemed to appear and disappear. But she knew it was still there, just a few blocks away, spinning over the neighborhood. A tornado!

Jessica took a quick photo. Wendy could see her friend's hand shaking.

Mrs. Stuard leaned into the microphone. "Everyone stand. Beginning with the back row, move quickly but orderly into the hallways. Duck and cover."

Wendy's heart pounded. She turned her head quickly and her glasses slid down her nose. She grabbed for them as everyone moved around her. Some of the kids were grinning and shoving each other like it was a game. But most of the kids moved quietly, their eyes wide.

The teachers quickly lined everyone against the walls and told them to squat on the floor.

"Heads down, arms folded over your head," Mr. Andrews repeated.

Wendy felt the air around them seem to push against her. A noise surrounded the school.

"Hey," Austin said. "What's that? There's no train around here."

Wendy shouted, "Duck and cover, Austin!" as the tornado she had dreaded moved above the school.

CHAPTER 9

Tornado!

Wendy had always wondered what it would be like to be in a tornado. But now she wished she'd only seen it in movies and news videos.

It seemed like she was in a room filled with a thousand speakers playing recordings of trains and crashing waterfalls. Glass shattered from down the hall.

The cafetorium!

Wendy hoped everyone was safely out. It had all happened so fast. It had been raining and dark one minute, then suddenly sunny and still.

Jessica leaned closer against her.

The sound of wind whistled all around them. Was this how Dorothy felt sitting on her bed in *The Wizard of Oz*?

Something crashed against the outside door down the hall. Maybe it was part of the playground equipment. Or the big oak tree in front of the school. Would the roof above them hold up?

Even Wendy screamed when another loud crash came from the direction of the cafetorium. What was happening in there?

"Will we be okay?" Austin shouted.

Wendy peeked through her arm at Austin, who was curled up in a tight ball. He was a jokester in class, but now Wendy felt sorry for him. She knew all about tornadoes, and she was even scared. He must be terrified.

"One hundred bottles of frogs on the wall, a hundred bottles of frogs!" Wendy sang loudly.

Dennis snorted. "Frogs?" he said in a muffled voice.

"Come on, help me," Wendy said. "Everyone is scared."

"Take one down, pass it around, a hundred bottles of frogs on the wall!" Dennis shouted.

After a moment, other kids joined in. Soon, Wendy could hear muffled voices singing up and down the halls.

She could still hear the sirens outside. The wind howled. Noises came from all around. Things pounded against the door at the end of the hall.

Wendy wanted to scream for the sounds to stop, but she kept singing.

"Eighty-seven bottles of frogs on the wall, eighty-seven bottles of frogs . . ."

And then, the pounding on the door stopped. The howling of the wind stopped. And finally, the sirens stopped.

In the middle of "seventy-nine bottles of frogs," the singing quieted.

"Listen," Jessica said. "I hear birds."

Wendy looked up. Everyone sat still as statues.

Finally, Mr. Andrews turned up the weather radio. " . . . the tornado warning for Tarrent, Dyson, and Clairmont counties has expired. Counties East; Dumont and Bradford are under a tornado warning and advised to take shelter immediately."

Wendy realized she had been holding her breath. She hoped the schools in the other cities were ready for the storms, too.

CHAPTER 10

Sharing the Plan

"Can we check out the cafetorium?" Jessica asked. "I should take some pictures of the mess."

Mr. Andrews shook his head. "We'll all sit here until Mrs. Stuard says it's safe to go back to our classrooms. She and the security officers are checking them out right now."

He had his school walkie-talkie in his hand. He gave the weather radio back to Dennis. "Thanks for bringing this to school. I'll get one for our classroom."

Dennis grinned. "Could we also get our own science lab?"

Mr. Andrews shook his head. Then Mrs. Stuard's voice squawked over the walkie-talkie.

"Please take your students back to their classrooms. There is a lot of glass in the first and second grade rooms, so please take your students to the gym. Parents are being notified to pick up their children as soon as possible. Please check everyone for injuries."

Mr. Andrews stood and motioned his class to follow him.

As soon as they got to class, Wendy ran to the windows. She was glad to see theirs hadn't been broken. But when she peered outside, she could see tree limbs all over the school yard. One of the see-saws was sitting in the driveway where the buses usually waited.

"Wow," Jessica said. She pulled her camera from her pocket and started taking pictures.

After he made sure no one had been hurt, Mr. Andrews sat at the class computer. "From what the weather service says, we probably had an F1 tornado hit this area. There's no major damage in town, but even an F1 can be dangerous. I'm proud of Wendy, Jessica, and Dennis. They helped us know what to do."

A cheer went up from Mr. Andrews's class.

Austin rolled his eyes, "Who's scared of a little wind?"

But when Wendy looked at him, he gave her a thumbs-up.

Everyone talked about the tornado while they waited for their parents. Some said they had been scared. Some said they weren't. Some wanted to sing about bottles of frogs on the wall again.

Wendy took out her notepad and wrote down what it felt like being in a tornado.

Mrs. Stuard came into the room and walked over to Wendy. "I can't thank you and your friends enough. I know I should have made a safety plan sooner. I'm going to suggest to the superintendent that we have a special meeting for all the school principals. We'll make sure everyone has a safety plan."

Wendy smiled. "My dad says that being prepared for extreme weather is extremely smart."

Mrs. Stuard nodded. "Well, you've proven he's right about that. I'd like you and your friends to come to this meeting. You can tell them how you checked out the school and found the weak and strong safety areas."

"We could tell them how to have a drill like we did here," Wendy suggested.

Mrs. Stuard agreed. When she walked away, Wendy hurried to where Dennis and Jessica were looking at the information on Mr. Andrews's computer. "You'll never believe what we get to do."

When she told them Mrs. Stuard's plan, Dennis let out a whoop. "I could show them some of my experiments. We'll be famous!"

Jessica held up her camera. "I can make an album of the school before and after the tornado. I still have pictures I took to show Mrs. Stuard the safe places in the school."

"Great idea," Wendy said. "We can show them why certain places in the school aren't safe and others are. Most people think all bathrooms are safe, but not if they are against an outside wall."

Jessica pointed her camera all around the room. "I'm going to interview some of the kids and teachers and take their pictures, too."

"By the time we're done, those principals will be begging us to come to their schools and help them the way we helped Mrs. Stuard," Wendy said. She wondered if they would let her bring Cumulus. He was part of their club.

Wendy snapped her fingers. It was time their club had a name.

"Wendy!" a voice called.

Wendy turned to see her mom standing at the classroom door. Wendy ran across the room and hugged her.

"Is everything okay at home? Is Cumulus okay?" Wendy asked.

Her mother nodded. "We just got some wind and rain. Everything at home is fine. I'm just so glad you all are safe. I told Dennis's and Jessica's parents I'd take them home, too."

Outside the school, Wendy and her friends followed her mom to the car. They walked past the Circleville Elementary cafetorium. All of the glass was shattered. Chairs were laying everywhere. One of the outside benches was upside down on the stage.

Wendy could see part of the ceiling hanging down.

"That's where we would have been sitting," Jessica said.

When they drove past the school, Dennis pointed out the mailbox that had been pulled up and tossed high up in a tree. There were fences laying around yards and in the streets.

Jessica snapped lots of photos.

Dennis whistled. "My tornado in a jar sure couldn't do that."

Wendy had a feeling that the other school principals would pay attention to what she and her friends had to say about weather safety.

CHAPTER 11

Heroes Get a Name

It was almost a week before the cafetorium and damaged classrooms at Circleville Elementary were fixed. Everyone spent the week going to school at Dragon Heights Elementary.

"It's not fair," Austin said. "We should get a tornado vacation."

But when they were all back at Circleville, everything seemed like normal again.

Mr. Andrews made them do math problems every day. Austin made wisecracks. And Bob the Boa escaped twice.

But it wasn't like normal when Mrs. Stuard made an announcement that there would be a special assembly in the cafetorium the last thirty minutes of school.

"What do you think it is?" Dennis asked.

Jessica shrugged. "They probably want to dedicate the new cafetorium or something."

Later that afternoon when everyone was seated, Mrs. Stuard raised her hand for quiet. Wendy saw a man and a woman on the stage with the principal.

"I'd like to introduce Mayor Rebecca Driscoll and Fire Chief Gabe Johnson. They have a little announcement to make."

Wendy leaned forward. She'd never seen a mayor before.

Mayor Driscoll looked just like someone's mother. She moved a curly piece of hair out of her eyes.

"I'm proud to be here at the reopening of Circleville Elementary," Mayor Driscoll said. "From what I've heard, you all did a great job of following instructions when the tornado hit. Because of your cooperation, each of you is responsible for the safety of your classmates."

She continued, "But, there are three students who did an extra special job of making sure every student at Circleville was safe. We'd like to recognize these special heroes."

Wendy gasped. Mrs. Stuard spoke into the microphone, "Will Wendy Peters, Dennis Galloway, and Jessica Roberts please come up front."

Wendy's heart pounded. She stood and followed her friends. Suddenly, she was standing beside the mayor!

The fire chief reached into a bag and pulled out three framed certificates. "We'd like to present this special safety award to each of you."

Wendy thanked him as he placed the award in her hand. Then the mayor shook their hands and smiled at them. A reporter from the *Circleville Times* took their photo.

Mrs. Stuard said, "I'm proud to say that these three students helped our school fight the tornado like warriors."

Wendy snapped her fingers. "That's it!" she shouted.

"What's it?" Dennis asked.

"Our club name," Wendy said. "The Weather Warriors."

Jessica gave her camera to Mrs. Stuard. She grouped her friends together. Then, they all held up their certificates for a photo.

"Wendy's Weather Warriors," Jessica added as Mr. Andrews snapped their picture.

Their club had a name. A perfect name. Wendy smiled as big as a Texas twister.

A funnel formed over water is called a waterspout. A funnel formed over a desert is called a dust devil. Neither of them is as strong as a tornado.

Usually, in the Northern Hemisphere tornadoes turn counterclockwise, and in the Southern Hemisphere they turn clockwise.

Tornadoes can happen almost everywhere in the world, but most happen in the United States. There, tornadoes are most common in an area called Tornado Alley. This area is from central Texas up to the Dakotas and across to Illinois.

Tornadoes can happen at any time of the year. In Tornado Alley, they most often appear in the spring.

Tornado Myths

MYTH: Windows should be opened before a tornado approaches. This will equalize the pressure and cause less damage.

FACT: Opening windows allows debris from a tornado to enter a building. Leave the windows shut and take cover in a safe place immediately.

MYTH: If you are in a car in a tornado, it's safe to park under an overpass and hide under the bridge for shelter.

FACT: This has been found to be dangerous. By sitting in your car, you are more likely to be hit by debris because you are higher up. It is better to lie in a ditch or somewhere flat than to climb up under a bridge where the tornado's wind is stronger.

DENNIS'S Favorite Experiments

BUILD AN ANEMOMETER

An anemometer is an instrument that measures wind speed. The spinning discs on a professional anemometer link to an electronic device. That device counts the turns and converts them into wind speeds. How can you measure wind speed?

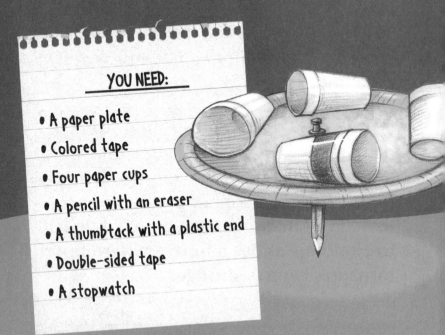

YOU NEED:

- A paper plate
- Colored tape
- Four paper cups
- A pencil with an eraser
- A thumbtack with a plastic end
- Double-sided tape
- A stopwatch

First mark one paper cup by wrapping the colored tape around the outside. With the pencil draw an 'x' on the plate. Try to get the middle of the 'x' as close to the middle of the plate as you can.

Then put a short piece of double-sided tape on the side of each of the four cups. Attach one cup to the edge of the plate (the opening of the cup must face left). Turn the plate and attach the rest of the cups the same way.

Punch the thumbtack through the middle of the plate, right where the 'x' marks the spot! Pin the plate to the eraser on the pencil and hold up the plate and cups so they can spin in the wind.

Check a local weather Web site to find the wind speed in your area. When you hold the homemade anemometer in the wind, count how many times the marked cup goes around in 30 seconds. Write it down. Do this at different times for several days. You are able to translate your numbers into wind speeds.

Indoor Tornado Experiment

Make your own whirling, spiraling tornado. No need to take cover from this fun and easy tornado creation!

YOU NEED:

- Food coloring
- A clear glass jar with a lid
- Water
- Liquid dish soap
- Vinegar

Fill your jar about two-thirds full with water. Choose a color and add a few drops of food coloring to the water. Next add a teaspoon of liquid dish soap and a teaspoon of vinegar. Make sure the lid is put on tightly! Shake the jar good and hard, but don't let go. Then give it a quick twist so the liquid will spin.

Ta-da! You're watching a tiny twister in a jar!